Alina
and Her Psychic Dog

D1810390

Sam Ramani

outskirts
press

This book is dedicated to my revered Guru
Sri Chandrasekara Saraswathy
Without whose blessings it would not have been possible.

ஸ்ரீ சந்திரசேகர சுவாமிகள் (ஸ்ரீ காஞ்சி பெரியவர்) ஸ்ரீ காமாக்ஷியம்மன் மூலஸ்தானம்

Preface

This book is a series of conversations between a girl belonging to the millennial group and her psychic dog. It tries to convey a different dimension to the problem of human interaction with the animals we live with and our rapidly depleting environment.

After reading this book, if everyone becomes more compassionate and humane towards the creatures that live with them on this planet earth, I would have been more than rewarded. Man has been living on this earth for more than a million years. The earth resources have been depleted by man over the centuries through his reckless actions, knowingly and unknowingly. Through this book, I hope to convey to the readers that animals that live with us have their psyches and emotions and suffer pain like humans. I know that man has used domesticated chickens, pigs, and cattle for his daily food source since the beginning of the world. In the beginning, humans killed animals for food only for their day to day needs. These actions preserved the balance in the environment.

Cattle were put in cages to fatten them, with hardly any room for their movement. They are fed fattening hormones and vitamins, which are harmful to people who consume them. In today's mass commercial cultivation of such animals for the food source, we have overlooked the simple compassion concepts. And the understanding that animals also feel pain and suffering like humans. Also, we are destroying the environment with excessive use of resources like water, which is already in short supply for our daily use in many parts of the world. The earth's resources are finite, and continued depletion of water to raise cattle will put us in an untenable position by the next decade. A typical steer uses more than 122,000 gallons of water till it's time to slaughter. With the advent of organic farming and free-range concepts, things have improved a little on this front and hopefully we will see a long term change over the next decade. I sincerely hope that with the new awareness in compassionate killing more and more people will reduce their dependency on meat daily and substitute the need for meat with alternative products like pasta, tofu, diet at least two to three times a week. (Since my writing this, alternative meat products like Beyond Meat and Impossible Burgers, have come to market) This slight modification in their eating habits will be more healthy in the long run for the people who adopt this new concept in diet and also help preserve the environment over a more extended period for our future generations.☺

Chapter 1
Early Life

I can see the sun hitting my bedroom through the windows and remembered today is a Saturday, and I don't have school. So I don't need to get up early. So I could sleep a little bit more. Today is a lazy day but, I will go with Natalya to the riverfront later to play. I can hear my grandmother calling my name, "Alina, come and have your breakfast." I loved my grandmother. She tells me stories from the Russian history of the brave men and women who fought in world war and stories from mythology. My grandmother is a psychic; she can see things in the future. She told me stories about the mystic Rasputin who lived long ago and scared away wolves staring at them when they came to attack him. And about the great Czars and Princesses who lived in Russia before.

We are a small family of four, myself, my parents, my grandmother, and we lived in Nizni Novogorod, a beautiful town north of Moscow. During the spring, flowers of different colors bloom. During summer, we have long days when we spend time on the riverfront and short nights. My father is a lecturer in Anthropology at the local university. My mother works in a medical clinic as an assistant.

My grandmother used to dream in the night, and at the breakfast table, she told me what the dream was every day. It was usually some relative popping in, usually my mother's brother, my uncle, whom I am very fond of.

During the week on regular days, I used to go to school with my friends walking. I come back at around 3 PM. My grandmother gives me a piece of cake and tea, and my friend Natalya comes to my house to play. In the summer days, we go to the riverside to play with some of the other girls. We have dinner around 7 PM as soon as my father comes home. I do my homework for an hour until 8 PM. My grandmother reads a book about fairytales. Sometimes she talks about the distant past.

She used to say that elephant-like animals called Mammoths lived in the northern parts of Russia thousands of years back. They moved in large herds. And they all perished when the ice-age came to Europe. And even a long time before that, animals used to speak and, some people understood them. She used to recall how, when she was a little girl, her grandmother used to tell her about war stories. During the Worldwar II, the Germans invaded Russia how the brave people in the western-front locked themselves in and resisted the German advance. When winter came, the soldiers did not have any food to eat, and many of them perished in the severe Russian winter. And eventually, the German forces retreated, and the war ended with the Allied troops (American-British-) winning back Europe from the Germans.

My grandmother also talked about the great Czars and Princesses of Russia, who had lived during her time. She also spoke about the great psychics who lived in the past and the present.

One evening when I came back from the riverfront, there was a visible commotion in the house. My mother was talking excitedly with my father about something. I learned that my father had received a teaching fellowship from the famous University of California at Berkely, USA. He was to report for duty in September. So we had to move to America in August. It was a big move for us, and I was excited about going to America.

My grandmother was not coming as she liked to stay in Russia with my uncle. I thought I was going to miss her sorely.

Chapter 2
Ancient Myths

My parents moved to the USA from Russia when I was twelve years old. We lived in San Francisco. I love this city, but what I miss most is my grandparents with whom I used to interact every day! I fondly remember my grandmother telling me bedtime stories almost every day till I was six years. I used to hear about the princess of Russia and their stories. But, what intrigued me most was the fact that my grandmother telling me that long ago, humans used to understand animals and birds speak. In fact, in ancient Egyptian and Indian legends, there is a mention of a special place for snakes. In one of the ancient Indian mythologies, Ramayana, that happened 10,000 years back, there is a story about how Rama, the exiled king, was helped by Men like Apes(half human and half Apes) to find his kidnapped wife. (These were an extinct group of primates that lived 12-14 million years before and were considered to be ancestors of modern humans). Their remains were found in India, and one of Rama's able assistant Hanuman the monkey god is still worshipped in India today.

In the ancient Hindu scripture called Bhagavata Purana, there is a reference to Lord Vishnu speaking to the first King Manu in the form of a fish warning him of an impending Apocalypse of rain and floods, that will end the world. He told him to make a big boat and populate it with one of each set of animals in the big boat before the Apocalypse and he will come in the form of a whale to lead his boat to safety. (compare this to the story of Noah's Ark in the bible which came much later!).

My grandmother was a psychic, and she used to have dreams about everything that was going to happen to us and others. I remember my dad was very anxious about our visa papers as they were unduly getting delayed, and my grandmother had a dream in which she saw a brown en-velope with an Eagle emblem delivered the next day. Sure enough, it was an envelope from the US embassy with a visa.

Like that, she had several dreams about events in our family that usually came true. I always thought about my grandmother and missed her terribly. But still, the thought of understanding animal speak vaguely intrigued me and was in the back of my mind. Soon I got busy with my high school preparation and pushed this idea to the back burner, and I thought, I will deal with it later at a convenient time.

Chapter 3
Talking Animals?

While I was busy with my school, I thought I would ask my history teacher, what my grandmother had said. One day after the class, I approached her very shyly and asked her what my grandmother had told me about the Animal-speak. To my surprise, she replied, "Honey, your grandmother told you legendary stories when you were young. I have heard, in Russia, there are many people with paranormal abilities like Rasputin who could control animals just by staring at them. But I have not heard of anyone understanding Animal-speak'. I assured myself that she did not think I was crazy or something to talk about Animal-speak.

I soon finished high school and got admitted to the University of CA at Berkely. I was a day student because my parents wanted to see me every day, and my schedule was rigorous. I found the Berkely university had a great library of all kinds of historical records about ancient civilization. I delved into them to find out if there was any reference to 'Animal-speak'. Although I found some references to the domestication of animals in ancient Egypt and Messapatomia, I did not find any specific reference to it in any of the literature. I was busy with my course work and did not give much thought to it, and also I did not have the time to devote to that.

I soon finished my course and got a job in a Bay Area pharmaceutical company. I took an apartment in San Francisco and started my life as a single professional woman. My parents were nearby and, I used to be in touch with them over the weekends. When I came home from work, I was feeling bored and lonely. So I thought of getting a dog that could keep me busy in the evening going for a walk etc. So in the weekends, I started scouting around the local pounds for an adoption. I saw a flyer that said the SPCA was doing adoption clinics in my area that weekend. This perked my interest and I decided to visit the clinic that weekend. There were a number of cute little puppies ranging from 6 weeks to 2 years and some older ones too. One beige puppy attracted my attention and he was looking at me intensely and I felt as though he was saying 'Take me, Take me, you wont lose on me!' Suddenly I felt a strange attraction to this puppy. With its focused look towards me I decided to move forward in adopting him. Normally I would have thought about this and then made a decision but something overrode my normal decision making process. The volunteer who helped me with this told me they call him Lawrence and said I could give my name if I wanted. I thanked her for her help and took him home. I made a temporary bed in a cardboard box and put him near the furnace to keep him warm in the night.

Chapter 4

Talking Dreams

We got used to each other, and I could understand most of the times what he wanted. I came home in the evening and he was happy to see me. Sometimes I used to take him for a walk after my dinner. I usually sat on the couch watching TV or reading a book.

One night I was reading a book on my couch and Lawrence was sitting right across me, his eyes focused on me, and his ears perked. Normally I have seen dogs when they sit down from across you; they usually have their head and eyes down. But Lawrence had his head raised and his ears perked. I thought it was unusual. Pretty soon, I fell asleep.

Suddenly I started hearing Lawrence talking in my dreams. He started saying

"You think I am some dumb dog? I chose you because I know you are psychic, and I will be able to communicate with you. I have a heavy load, which I want to get off my chest. I wanted to confess something terrible, which I have done in my previous life.

I was a doctor in Ukraine in my previous life, and I was very greedy for money and became careless in treating my patients. I once operated on a 14-year-old girl, which ended up in her paralysis for life due to my carelessness. There were too many other instances where I let down people who trusted me with their lives.

Towards the end of my life, I felt remorseful, and I thought I will have a terrible end of life with a serious illness. So I started doing good actions, helping charities, giving my money to the needy, and doing similar deeds. When that did not happen, I thought I was blessed! I knew I had to pay for these misdeeds somehow somewhere. Little did I know then that I will be born as a dog in this life. So I decided to be an 'activist' dog, meaning I will try to do something good to change existing conditions for animals.

Fear before Killing

When I woke up, it was past midnight and Lawrence was still in the same place looking at me as though he has done something. I went to bed wondering whether what I had experienced was real or dream of having a psychic experience? But the whole thing felt surreal that I thought I have no way of verifying what was happening to me. I thought maybe it is a freak incident and did not know what to make of it.

The next day I was busy with something and worked late before going to bed. The day after, as usual I came back from the walk with Lawrence and sat on my couch reading a book. Lawrence was very perky and I thought maybe the incident will repeat itself. This time I decided if it happened I would try to talk back to him. Sure enough I fell into a nap and was startled by the dream and Lawrence started to talk to me again. He started with asking

'Do you remember what I said last time?

Me: I said, Yes I remember. How can I help you?

'Well for starters, you can become a vegetarian.'

Me: Why so?

Have you seen how they kill the animals for your meat?

Me: No, but I have not thought about it.

They bludgeon the pigs to death for your bacon.

They are housed in cages and fatten them with hormones. They can hardly move left or right in the track they are in. They lie in their feces even after they are killed and you end up eating that end product!

Do you know you will feel extreme pain when somebody hits you on the head?

Me: Yes, they have to be killed to be eaten.

But you don't have to beat them to death before eating them.

The cattle know intuitively before they are killed, and they become very agitated. I have seen lambs before being taken to slaughter house in my country, get very agitated. They refuse to come down from the van in which they are brought to the slaughter house. They are usually dragged down by force. They know they are going to die.

Me: So what are you saying? You cannot kill any animals?

I am trying to make a case for killing animals compassionately that will be painless for them. Maybe, through an injection. When you kill them with brute force, they are in extreme fear, and that usually gets into their psyche. Those who eat that meat will have that fear psychosis transferred to them and that will become part of their psyche.

Me: Okay I understand your point but how does my becoming a vegetarian help that cause?

The less people eat meat, less killing has to be done and we will save the environment also by saving water and other resources used to raise the cattle.

Me: Okay, I will try to cut down on my meat- eating.

Once you do that and think about where it is coming from, you will probably stop eating it completely! You will also save yourself from breast and colon cancers.

Me: So how do I get my protein if I am a vegetarian?

You can replace it with alternative plant-based products, that will give you enough protein.

Chapter 5
Pain & Emotions of Animals

I was thinking about what Lawrence had said. I understood the argument he made and thought there was some merit in what he was saying. So I thought how I could reduce my consumption of red meat and chicken-based products. I visited the local whole foods store and checked the availability of plant-based protein products. I found lots of alternatives like plant-based burgers, sausage links, bacon strips, and protein shakes. So I decided to substitute my diet with plant-based proteins. The next session was more subdued. I thought I will test his memory and find out more about his previous lives. The conversation went like this

Me: 'Do you remember your previous lives?

Yes dear, I was a flamenco dancer in Catalunya, Spain. I belonged to the Romany tribe, and I did lots of good things for my community. Since we were discriminated a lot by the local people, my people were suffering a lot. I contributed generously to the upliftment of my people by funding kids for education, housing and food for the deserving etc.

Maybe due to these good deeds, I was born as a doctor in my last life.

Me: What about before that? Do you remember it?

Yes, dear I was a worker at the Vatican and I saw all of the luxury and lavishness that was there. All the day to day stuff goings on. It was an eye-opener for me as to how public money can be spent for the good and wasteful things. I will tell you about my experiences there another time. It will be exciting!

Dear Alina, I want to talk about my life when I was a Flamenco dancer. That is when I learned about emotions and pain. As a Flamenco dancer, I often got the front seat to all the Bull Fight performances. I used to see the Matador going through the motions and finally gore the bull. The poor bull lay there writhing in pain with a neck wound kicking its legs and making me sick in the stomach, while thousands cheered! Soon I stopped going to this mass entertainment because I could not see the bull in pain. This used to haunt me through the nights, seeing the bull's image in pain before dying.

I had an opportunity to go for a performance in Africa. During the off time, we were taken for a safari. There I saw a very poignant scene. A cheetah with two cubs was shifting her den because she sensed danger to her den. She could carry only one cub at a time so she carried the first one to the interior. While she was gone a jackal carried away the cub that was in the den. The cheetah returned to the den and looked for it's missing cub. She looked desolate with pain in her face as she looked around for her cub grunting. She was totally devastated and I could see she was feeling pain for the loss of her cub. That moment something dawned on me about animals also feeling pain like humans.

Animals are very intuitive about death, and they know they are being taken to the slaughter house. In Ukraine my clinic was in on the 2nd floor, and across the street was the slaughter house in the backside. I could see them unloading sheep and goats from a closed van, and they usually take them to the back of the building through the side. I could hear, when the driver opened the back of the van, the goats and sheep wailing and they had to be literally dragged out of the van and the driver had to drag them all the way while they were wailing loudly. On checking with my staff I found that they were being taken to the slaughter house. These wailings are not the usual bleats emitted by them under normal circumstances. They are usually the wail of death knowing they were going to be killed..

Have you been near someone who is about to die? They emit a similar sound when the 'Prana' or the life force leaves them when they die. I had occasion to hear a similar sound from a close relative of mine. My cousin brother who was much younger, was 50 years old. He had some heart issues, which he did not take care of properly. So on that fateful day, we had a nice dinner in a restaurant having some small talk. At the end of the dinner, while we were having coffee; suddenly he started shaking violently. I thought he was choking and got behind him and tried to shake him and do a Heimlich maneouver. He collapsed with a sound that was same as the goat wailing at the time of death 'blaaaah' in a low wailing voice. This is the sound, when the life force Prana leaves the body. It is the same wailing sound emitted by a sheep when it's throat is cut.

I have told you all this. It is time to pause and ask you a question. Do you think animals feel pain like humans?

Alina: Probably so. I have never thought about it deeply.

What gives you the right to deny us our natural right to procreation? Do you think it is easy to live as a neutered dog?? Think about it. What if it is done to you when you were a kid and you never experienced the joys of motherhood and off springs?

Alina: Come to think of it, I think it is a wrong thing to do. The next day when I was taking Lawrence for a walk I thought about what he said about neutering. I felt it was wrong to do it but I did not have any answers.

Chapter 6

The Universal Law

The next session was two days later which was a Friday. I had a hard day at work, and was looking forward to a nice relaxing Friday night watching some TV and I started dozing off in the couch and I had a session from Lawrence. He continued

"Have you ever hit yourself on the head with a rolling pin really hard? I don't think we will do it because it will pain. What do you think a pig feels when it is bludgeoned on the head to death? Extreme fear! The extreme fear, when it is dying, is transferred to the resulting meat, people eat. This is transferred to the humans who eat this pig with serious repercussions on their mental and physical health.

Let me tell you about the Universal Law. This is the law which governs everything we think, do and all our actions. Your thoughts are put in the universe, and they can be picked up by someone else in the universe here or somewhere else. Sometimes if your thoughts are so powerful, someone else can pick up your thoughts, and if the conditions are right, they can act upon it. And if your mind is powerful, you can control someone else. Likewise, your actions or 'karma' has consequences like a ping pong ball. It will bounce off from one person to another, and many people can be affected by it. Sometimes it is like a domino effect.

I will give you an analogy for this. Imagine you have a bag of bird seeds that are weightless and can fly in the air. You throw a handful into the air, and they are scattered. They can land anywhere on trees, on the ground, on the water, etc. A seed that falls on the ground will be dormant. Watch that word. It will be beneficial to understand karma. The dormant seed can lay in the ground for a year or two until the ground conditions become okay for the seed to germinate. Karma works the same way. It remains dormant sometimes for several after-lives or sometimes will fructify in this life itself if the conditions permit. Your thoughts and actions is your karma and it always stays with you in this life or your afterlife. It remains part of your psyche till it gets worked out in one of the lives.

There is one more attribute that goes with you, other than your karma. These are pent up desires you acquire in a lifetime called 'Vasanas'; they remain with you in the after-life, till you work them out. A simple example is your craving for one type of food or for sex. You have to try to work these pent up desires out in this life; then they won't follow you in your next life if the vasana is exhausted.

I will give another example of a business executive who

never made any decisions. He used to postpone making decisions and procrastinate on every decision. Finally, he became a basket case and could not run his business because he kept postponing everything. Unfortunately, he died of a heart attack and will have to work out this attribute in his next life. It will continue to haunt you in every new life till you work it out. To work out this attribute (I am talking about only negative ones that seems to impede one's growth), you need to become aware of it first through self-introspection. Once you identify them, it will be easy for you to get them out of your system.

Meditation is the only vehicle to identify them and slowly burn them out over time. Meditation allows you to look at yourself inward and get in touch with your psyche or known as 'Consciousness' in the eastern religion.

Chapter 7

The Silent Mind &
Power of Consciousness

There are also the right side of 'vasanas', one of which is meditation. If you start meditation in this life, you will surely pick it up where you left off, in your next life, which will be a progression for you in the evolution ladder. This is something we should be thankful about.

Meditation allows you to silence your mind. When your mind is truly silent, you will become aware of the life force inside you.

You can take control of your life force and parlay it as you please. This force is known as the 'Force of Aurobindo' (an Indian mystic who lived in the 1890s-19th century). He demonstrated it to one of the skeptics. He was an Englishman who wanted to investigate Aurobindo's 'Silent Meditation' He was asked to wait in his hotel room at an appointed time. Aurobindo's companion also known as the 'Mother', was in another building. She parlayed this force's power on the Englishman, and he started shaking violently and sweating profusely for a few minutes till the force lasted. After this demonstration, he was totally convinced of the power of the force that comes from silencing of the mind.

A silent mind is like an antenna that can receive all the vibrations around, and you can selectively receive or block these vibrations. In this way, you can also read other people's thoughts.

Through meditation, one can get in touch with one's consciousness; once you do that, your consciousness will take control of your life and take you through various paths which you would not have been able to do by yourself, under normal circumstances. Sometimes it can expedite one's karma in this life. That is why you will see some persons going through multiple tragedies in this life in quick succession. Sometimes you will see persons who will lose every relation they have and will be left alone to deal with being alone. That person was probably afraid to be alone by herself all her life.

If you think about it deeply you will find that your relationship with other people will end abruptly sometimes. It is because your previous life's connection with that person will be over at that time. Your connections with people in this life is like in a train journey. You meet people and as soon as you reach your station, you have to get off and the people you knew in the train go their own way and you may not see them again. Your life on earth this time is like that. When your station comes you have to leave and your jiva moves on to another body.

I will tell you about consciousness, which is an independent, self-sufficient force residing in every body, humans, animals, plants and inanimate objects. In most humans this force is hidden inside you. Under normal circumstances your mind acts as a screen to block it, so rarely you will be able to know it is even present in you! Sometimes for a split second you can feel it when you look at enormous beauty like the ocean with sun shining on it. Then it disappears. I think the purpose of human birth is to become aware of your consciousness so that you can progress on the ladder of evolution. It takes a monumental effort for you to be aware of it. For that you have to bypass the mind. The way you bypass your mind is to make it 'silent'. That requires practice. Through meditation one can silence the mind and get in touch with your consciousness. Once you are able to do it, you have this tremendous power to overcome all obstacles and do something creative. Great deeds can be accomplished through the contact with one's consciousness.

When the life force 'prana' (Sanskrit) that made your body alive leaves you, your body is a mass of worthless flesh. Even vermins and birds will not eat this mass of disintegrated flesh after a few days. The consciousness that was hidden under your mind made your body full of vitality, with your blood flowing to your face with your smiles, become non-existant when the Prana leaves. What a sudden contrast! Your time in this life has ended. That is why I do not understand why some Christian religions of the west embalm their saints and preserve their bodies for ages which is a futile exercise as there is nothing in the bodies. I know of one such church in Kiev (Ukraine) known as the Lavra Caves where in underground caves bodies of monks who lived 800 years before are still preserved. Similarly there are other churches in Europe where some of the saints' bodies are preserved.

In our daily life we often encounter people who are capable of extraordinary feats. These are feats normally above the ordinary. They stand out as great accomplishments. Like an artist with a great painting, a musician with a great composition, a scientist with a new discovery, etc. Probably these people's consciousness was alive and they were in touch with them and it helped them to rise to those great levels of accomplishments.

Chapter 8

Stepping up on the Evolution Ladder

I will be amiss if I don't explain the role of life force (Prana in Sanskrit) in our lives.

Alina: I was intrigued by all the data overload from Lawrence and wanted to think about it more. Most of what he has been saying was new information for me. I did not know anything about what he was saying. Then again I had an open mind to it and wanted to learn as much as possible about what he was saying.

The next session from Lawrence happened after a week because we had a long weekend in between and I was busy with my house cleaning and other errands.

It was again a Friday and I was sitting on a couch and falling asleep after my dinner.

Lawrence: So we left off with the power of consciousness last. The bottom line for you to know is when one gets in touch with his/her consciousness, he/she becomes a different person. Later on that same person looks back and thinks how he did what he did. He is awed and knows a force bigger than him/her has helped him/her to do what he/she did. So what I am saying is, everyone should try to get into touch with their consciousness to evolve into the next step. Human life is different from that of the animals because humans are endowed with discrimination ability which animals do not have. Animals are propelled by their intuition and are focused on finding their food to satisfy their hunger for the moment.

The human birth is given to you due to your good actions (karma) in your past lives and provides you an opportunity to climb up the evolution ladder to the next step. If you did not do anything to advance yourself in this life, you will be born again and again in a similar life; man, animal, man etc. till you get into touch with your consciousness. When you get into touch with consciousness it will drive you towards your next level of evolution, and you do not stop then. You keep climbing the ladder until you reach the source of consciousness, a big ball of consciousness (also known as the Supreme Power, Supreme Deity, God, etc.) from which all life forms of the universe have originated as a spark. This consciousness is to reach the source from which it came, and it will constantly work to going towards it. In the process you will be stepping up the evolution ladder. After, many many births, animals will evolve into humans and man can go back as animals during this process. You can see in your everyday life around you. I know a friend, whose face resembles that of a bird, and I used to joke with her, that she was a bird in one of her previous lives. True to that she has such an affinity towards birds and she goes out of the way to feed them every day meticulously. This may be due to her previous birth connection and 'vasana' about which I talked before.

Chapter 9

Humane Killings

All these pronunciations from Lawrence were a little bit heavy for me to digest, as he was going into areas that were new territory hitherto unheard of by me. So I made some notes after the sessions and was unsure how I would do something about it. So I thought the best way is to ask him in the next session. So I was mentally prepared to ask him the question in the next session. The next session was after a week, and I was ready with my question.

Lawrence, you have told me all this information. How do you think I can help your cause?

Lawr: Well, as a first step you can join or help create an organization like SPCA, Humane Society, etc. to make people aware in a big away about stopping cruelty to animals and the practice of neutering pets, for which you have no moral authority. Who gives you the right to control the procreation of pets? It is like the Govt. telling a woman you cannot have any kids! Do you think they will accept it meekly?

Look what happened in China with their disastrous policy of one kid per family?

Female fetuses were aborted en masse resulting in a disproportionate ratio of young men to women. Similarly it was practiced in many of the Asian countries like India. Any country that practices willful infanticide will get evil 'group karma' with undesirable consequences for their people.

The fulfillment for animals in their lives is also through giving birth to their offsprings. Their consciousness evolves to the next stage through that. You are interfering in that process which is bad 'karma' for society.

Alena: What is the alternative to controlling the pet population? Surely, you are not saying that we should be stuck with millions of unwanted pets?

Law: I am not advocating that at all! All I am saying is 'do not prevent a female from experiencing a birth cycle'. This is their fulfillment in life. After one birth cycle, you can use birth control for the male or female to prevent unwanted births. Unfortunately, since you want to keep pets, you have to take on the additional responsibility of dealing with their births also.

Chapter 10
Out of Body

I am going to tell you now about another most misunderstood psychic phenomenon known as 'Out of Body' experience. It happened to me when I was a doctor in Ukraine in my previous life. I had a very busy day with lots of patients, and I was taking a break around three pm lying on my couch. I was very tired by then and dozed off unwittingly. Suddenly I felt my heart opening up with a thud, and I was flying around the room. After three rounds, I was back into my body, and I woke up startled. I had a distinct impression of what happened. I knew I had an out of the body experience. I was trying to trace back to remember what happened. I remember my mind was running behind my form trying to catch up with what was happening. This is the peculiar thing in out of body experiences. When you come out of your body (it is actually your form that is coming out while your physical body remains still or in deep sleep) your mind is trying to race and play catch up. You will be aware you are flying, but your conscious mind is playing catch up with your experience.

You must have heard of stories of people having near-death experiences when they are in a coma; or a patient coming out of his body in the operation theatre and looking from above while surgery is performed on him. The probable cause of this could be something like this. When the body is in severe trauma, your form suddenly gets ejected. The form is an exact copy of you and can see everything that is happening to you and around you. It is like a modern-day Drone with a camera. This form cannot stay too long outside and it will try to enter the body. I will tell you more about this form later when I tell you what happens when a person dies.

But one who has practiced this art or technique is able to stay longer outside. In early Indian literature around 1600 AD there is a story about the great mystic Sankara (1600AD) who re-established Hinduism in India over Budhism. He had to win a debate about Advaita philosophy of non-dualism (which he was espousing) with his opponent, who advocated Dualism. Sankara who was a celebate monk was disqualified because he did not have life's experiences as a married man (Grahastha in Sanskrit). He told his opponents that he will gain the experience of life as a married man, and will come back to continue the debate. He was reported to have gone to a cave in the Himalayas, where he asked his disciples (followers) to look after his body till he returned. He then went out of his body and entered the body of a king who was dying and continued the king's life for some time, till he gained the experiences of a married man. He then returned to his original body and went back to finish the debate over non-dualism. He estabalished the superiority of non-dualism as the main Hindu philosophy of Sanatana dharma.(there is only one and not two)

I have seen this ability run in families who are psychic or who get dreams or premonitions. My mother had this ability, and she used to talk about flying in the night to different places or visiting some of her close relatives and acquaintances. She used to tell with astounding accuracy as to what some of them were doing! We did not take her seriously, but later on I read some literature on it, and many books have been written on it. An old English book even tells you how one can develop this trait through practice. In my case, I am sure I got it from my mother, who was a psychic. I had this one clear experience that stood out from others that were dreams mostly in the night when I was asleep. From the literature, I have read of instances where a little girl in Paris was able to go out of her body every night and look down upon the town where she lived. She could see the streets of Paris lighted up. There are some techniques in meditation that lend itself to developing this ability. The OB is a detailed subject in itself and part of the various meditation techniques that are used for different outcomes.

There is one more phenomenon that is related to

this. Some people talk of seeing a light while they are in a coma. The out-of- body experience is usually mixed up with coma patients, who report seeing bright lights. This is the spent energy that moves through the human 'chakras '(the chakras are invisible points in various parts of the body, through which energy is channeled) gives out bright lights.

That was the end of the session for that night. It was lots of new information which I got and enough work for me to think about these things. The next session was a continuation of the chakras the following week.

Chapter 11
The Chakras

The chakras are energy nodes in the body where all energy channels of the body meet, and they are seven in number. They open and close depending on the the energy stimulation they receive. They are not physical nodes which we can see. They are part of the 360 energy channels in the body that sustain the body in the daily activities. Starting at the bottom of the vertebrae called Muladhara, next one in the prostatic area called Swadhistana, next Manipura behind the solar plexus (this is the main storage area for Prana, the Life Force), next Anahata in the heart area, next one Visudha in the throat area , next one Ajna between the eyes on the forehead, and the last one Sahasrara on the crown of the head. These Chakras have their own associated colors like Red for Manipura (solar plexus), blue for Visudha throat chakra, smoke-colored for Anahata, snow-white for Ajna between the eyes, white for Swadhisthana and yellow for Muladhara. This could explain why when someone goes into a coma, they see colored lights because some of the chakras open or close due to extreme stimulation from the life force, Prana. According to the Tibetan system, there are three main channels in the human body. They are the main energy channels. The Tibetan system has quantified these chakras and energy channels in detail and how they operate. The energy dormant in the lowermost chakra is latent, and called the 'Kundalini' It is coiled in the form of a serpent. In some cases, this energy can rise and go through activating all the chakras (nodes) and come out of the crown of the head through the Sahasrara chakra (also commonly referred as 1000 points of lights). At this point the person is considered to be fully liberated and have attained consciousness.

The Tibetan system recognizes three main channels of energy in the body, red channel (on the right side for women and left for men), white channel (left for women and right for men) and the central channel which is blue. We can visualize two thin pencils for the right and left channels and one thick pencil for the blue channel running from below the navel to the crown of the head and coming out of the nose. The red channels signify positive emotions while the white channels denote our negative emotions. The central channel is where the primordial energy resides, and the life force moves. In the night when we sleep, the mind goes through various chakras producing different types of dreams. We can intervene in that process and change the outcome of the dream by making Prana and the mind move in unison. This can be accomplished by constant practice of holding the Prana moving in the central channel. Great feats and accomplishments have been done by those with the Prana moving in their central channel. There is an extensive literature in Tibetan system on Dream Yoga and using the Prana in the central channel to become aware of the state between life and death and of one's passage to the next life. By constant practice we can channel the Prana in the central blue channel to take control of your dreams when you are asleep. This control over the Prana gives permanent awareness while passing from this life to the next state. This is according to the Tibetan concept of life and death.

Chapter 12

Dreams

There is a big emphasis on dreams in Tibetan daily life and culture. It is very normal for someone to say that he dreamt of some such thing or about his mother asking him to do something and others believe him. But dreams are mostly maligned in the west and the scientific community has not been able to answer the mechanics of dreams and paranormal activity.

There are many varieties of dreams that are classifiable as normal every night dreams which we forget next day, dreams that have a premonition factor attributed to them, dreams that are in nature of futuristic events told in advance, dreams from past life and the dreams that help you transition to the next life like in the Tibetan system.

The common dreams that everyone has and forget the next day is explained by science as follows:

When you go to sleep, your mind is at rest, and there is a subconscious mind that works. This subconscious mind gives vent to our suppressed desires that tends to come out when your mind is at rest. According to science everyone dreams and they are not aware of their dreams. Usually since dreams are abstract, they try to convey a message through objects of your association. So everyone has to interpret their dreams with their secondary association. For example if your sister denotes some particular attribute in your life, you will see her to denote that particular attribute. This is how your subconscious mind tries to convey a message through an abstract dream. This explanation falls short of explaining about premonition, seeing of events in the future, clairvoyance, telepathic communication, and other paranormal activities.

Some people have a built-in mechanism in their system that tends to warn them of an impending danger through a dream of premonition. Before Abraham Lincoln died, his wife had a dream of him getting shot. This was a protection mechanism of Lincoln's wife warning her of an impending danger. There are many instances in people's lives, where they have had premonitions of untoward things happen to them. I used to have a typical dream that always repeated when I was in some kind of problem with my work situation. The dream usually has someone with dark glasses chasing me, I am running away, and finally I climb a ladder to a rooftop and push the ladder out, and the dream ends. The first time I had this dream, I did not know what to make of it; but I had the answer next day. A Govt. health inspector was sitting in my office when I went to work. And he had received a complaint from one of my competitors about alleged mis-use of some drug. I showed him that was not the case, and he was thoroughly convinced and closed the case. Then I re-membered my dream and deciphered it as follows: the man chasing me with sunglasses – a Govt. official. Chasing me-was a complaint against me. My climbing on the rooftop and pushing the ladder- my escape from the situation. Strangely I used to get this dream whenever I had some issue with the Govt. and in all cases, I was able to take appropriate action to exonerate myself before the incident happened. This dream is a clear example of the inbuilt mechanism of protection against an upcoming adverse event.

There are passive dreams that simply try to tell you of an important upcoming event in your life. I had a recurring dream when I was young. Every night around midnight, I dreamt of bathing in a large pond that had long stone steps all around the pond. I used to wakeup after the dream. I had this dream almost every other night for six months. Even though I came from a family of psychics, I did not know what to make of it. Usually water indicates a journey in my dreams and I was planning a long trip out of my country at that time. So I thought the dream was referring to my travel. At the end of six months, I got a cable one day, saying my fa-ther had passed away suddenly due to an obstruction in his stomach. My father was very healthy, and he was in his six-ties and had no preconditions of any illness. I was naturally shocked and went to my town and to my amazement I saw the large pond nearby in which I had to take several baths. This dream could not be explained as a coincidence as I have never seen this pond before, and I had this dream recurring over six months.

The session ended with the promise to continue the topic of dreams in the next one.

Chapter 13

Anxiety Dreams

In the next session, Lawrence continued on the dream topic.

There is another kind of dream that creates or changes an existing situation in our lives. This is rare because most dreams only signify an event that is going to occur in the future, and very rarely, they are dynamic to change an existing situation.

In one of the Indian magazines, there was a report of a famous ophthalmologist of Mumbai whose wife was very religious. She died one day, and after a few weeks, she appeared at the house of her brother. He was shocked and scared. After a few weeks, his wife, who could not give birth due to some problem in her uterus, had a dream of her brother's sister who was telling her that she will be born as a girl to her, and she should be given her name to the child. In the dream, she asked her to go to a doctor and check for pregnancy. When she went to check, her doctor was stunned to find her pregnant! This type of dream is a combination of premonition and foretelling of a future event by a dead person and changing the outcome of an existing situation.

Then there are the 'anxiety dreams'. When you are in great anxiety about some problem in your life, a solution may appear in the form of a dream.

In the old Oxford University press, there was an interesting article about Sir Wallace who was a distinguished scholar in ancient Semitic languages. When he was in school, he showed excellent academic abilities in learning ancient languages, and he was admitted to Cambridge University. He could learn Assyrian well but had some difficulty with Accadian, the Semitic language. At that time there were only 3 or 4 people who knew these languages well in Europe. Once, a competition on ancient languages was organized by Cambridge University with scholarships for higher studies for the students who would pass in first-class rank. The principal of Christ Church College informed young Bas about this competition and encouraged him to participate, as he was impressed by his language learning abilities. The chief examiner of this competition was Professor Shetz, who was a scholar in ancient languages. And Bas had not the opportunity to hear his lectures or speak with him, so he was very worried about taking part in the competition. He was very nervous about the challenge, and his anxiety increased as the competition neared, despite his hard work and preparation. And he almost thought of dropping out of it the previous day. That night, when the anxious young Bas went to sleep, he had a dream. He was sitting in a room with one ventilator, and a teacher entered and pulled out an envelope from his coat pocket with green sheets of papers. He told him, 'Look you are to answer so many questions from this paper and translate this paragraph from Assyrian and Accadian languages into English' The examiner went out and locked the door behind him. Bas read the questions in his dream carefully, woke up from his sleep, freshened himself, and prepared for those questions. Nextday when he went for the exam, there was a big crowd and the exam hall was full. So he was directed to an adjacent room with a single ventilator, as he had seen in his dream. The examiner entered and pulled out the envelope and green sheets of paper and gave the same instructions to Bas as was in the dream and left the room locking it behind him.

Bas was stunned to see the same questions he had seen in the dream, and he was very well prepared to answer them. He came out of the competition with flying colors and got the scholarship for higher studies in Ancient Languages. He became a Professor of Ancient Languages and became the head of the department of Egyptian and Assyrian studies in the British Museum. This is a classic example of a dream providing you the solution when your mind is driven by a high level of anxiety.

Chapter 14
Telepathy in Dreams

Then there are dreams involving telepathy contact between two people who are in a highly charged emotional situation.

When I was in Ukraine I heard about a popular fascinating story of telepathy from Poland. Stanislas, a soldier, was engaged to be married to Marena in the town of Zarnak. Before a few days to their wedding, Stanislas was called by his battalion commander to report for duty in a distant town, due to the sudden development of war. So Marena's wedding was canceled. Stanislas promised, he will come back after the war to marry her. The war raged and many soldiers from his battalion died. And Stanislas was also reported missing. Marena could not take the news of the war, and she was highly emotionally charged. One night she had a dream about Stanislas. He was pale and in ragged clothes, and he was calling Marena to help him. He was trapped in a tunnel, and she could see candlelight. It was under a Mountain Fort. Next morning Marina was highly charged and excited. Again she dreamed of him in the tunnel. So she started telling her parents and her neighbors to do something about it. They all thought she needed psychiatric help and the father from her church, asked her to console herself with other activities. Everyone thought she was on the verge of madness due to his loss. After a few weeks again she saw the dream and now she was convinced he was alive. So she decided to take matters into her hands and search for the towns, where the war had taken place. There were many forts in Poland, but she did not give up. Finally she arrived in a remote village, where there was a fort on top of the mountain. She recognized that fort immediately and asked the local people to help her look in the fort for a tunnel. A policeman, who was local there, told her that he has been guarding this place, and there is no sign of any life under the fort. But Marina insisted her husband is there and with the help of some local people started taking out the stones. Finally, they saw a tunnel with candlelight inside. Two local people went inside the tunnel and brought Stanislas out. He was still living, but pale and distraught. He was incharge of a storeroom so, he could find some dry foods to keep him alive. Thus ended Marena's ordeal, and they were happily married. This incident is a classic case of two people communicating, while in distress and finding a solution to their problems through dreams, when others are helpless.

Then there is the type of dreams classified as Divine Dreams that foretells of a very important event about to happen. An example of one is of the Budha before he was born. His mother, Queen Maya had a dream that an elephant with a body stronger than iron, with six white teeth, white in color, more brighter than the sun and moon, had entered her body. She narrated the dream to her husband, King Shudhodhana who called the court astrologers to tell the meaning of the dream. The astrologers conferred and deciphered the dream as the symbolic birth of a great, enlightened and extraordinary soul, who will be king of all kings and, will be immortal.

There are several other documented cases of dreams of different types involving all of the paranormal phenomenon.

These examples of dreams, for which there is no real explanation in the scientific community, can be explained if we were to assume that the subconscious mind has another dimension to it. Remember, we talked about the chakras before and the Prana passing through them. When the mind is highly charged with anxiety, emotion or fear, the third dimension from your subconscious sends out signals to protect you, in the form of dreams and telepathic messages. The Indian and Tibetan scriptures have dissected the mind into subtle layers and each layer is capable of being stimulated by the Prana moving through the chakras. This comes out as impulses in the form of paranormal experiences. As per the Indian scriptures, the soul is a silent and constant witness to all these activities, in the waken and the dreaming state.

Chapter 15

Reincarnation

The next session continued as usual after a week in which Lawrence talks about Reincarnation or Life after Death.

I want to talk about another related topic which is Life after Death called Reincarnation. I do not need to believe whether it is true or not because evolved souls like Budha remembered their previous births, so know that there is life after this one. But I did not know about my last birth. The Eastern religions believed in that concept, especially in India &Tibet, where it is a firmly rooted belief. Though, today the western world dismisses it as unscientific, there are lots of instances where the reincarnation myth has been investigated and proved to be true. It has been done in Sri Lanka and India. Usually the persons who remember their previous births have had a traumatic end in their past lives like suddenly being killed violently or in an accident; they remember what happened to them and want to find closure to the grievous harm done to them.

I had a letter from a woman from Russia who had repeated dreams of her being a princess of a Maharaja (king) in India. While she was waiting for her lover in an emerald rose garden with sandalwood smell, she was murdered. So this incident comes as a dream for her in this life many times. Since this happened in India, I told her I would do some research and find out where this could have happened, as there are not too many Maharajas in India, and she could find closure for her dreams once I identify the place. I identified the palace, she was referring to which was in Mysore, India where a garden she described existed. I gave this information to her and asked her to go and find closure for her dreams.

Even though Indian scriptures abound with the concept of transmigration of the soul from one life to another, the earliest recorded rebirth is in the famous Indian epic Mahabaratha set in 5000 BC. Sometimes when we do not have the empirical evidence for an event, reliable historical record can form the basis of our conclusions.

In the story of Mahabaratha, Bheeshma, the invincible commander-in-chief of the Kaurava clan of Hastinapur, was killed by a transgender Shikandi from the Pandava clan and turned the course of the war. Shikandi was one of the Princess of Kasi in her previous birth, and had vowed to come back in her next birth and kill Bheeshma and avenge the insult done to her by Bheeshma. Bheeshma kidnapped her from her fiancée king and released her later when he came to know about her fiancee. When she went back to her fiancée, he refused to accept her, and she came back to Bheeshma and asked him to marry her. Bheeshma refused, saying he is a confirmed bachelor. So the princess vowed to avenge her insult in her next birth.

The next case is that of the Budha whose past lives were all chronicled in The Jataka Tales. In this chronicle all the Budha's past lives were described from animal and human births.

Indian scriptures of the Vedanta class has maintained the imperishableness of the soul and its transmigration from one life to another. This itself is a logical reason to assume there is life after death. It goes one step further with the concept of reincarnation, in which a person works out his 'karma' of previous lives in a next birth. (Karma is the fruit of actions or consequences of deeds done in one's life good and bad; the results of which will manifest in a next life) This is the main difference between life after death and reincarnation, where one is born in a next life with a specific purpose of working out his past karma.

In western paranormal science, attempts were made by many psychoanalysts like de Rochas (1911) to regress an 18 year old girl to age four and then to her past life.

When the regression went to past births, it failed to provide the required evidence either because the information provided was not verifiable or the subjects madeup the information. So the experiment with hypnotic techniques to verify reincarnation was abandoned as not being fruitful.

Stevenson, a University of Virginia Psychiatry Professor published the results of his extensive study done by him suggestive of reincarnation. Subjects who were mainly children were chosen from different countries of India, Sri Lanka, Brazil, Alaska and Lenabon. Stevenson investigated and recorded around 2500 cases very systematically, eliminating even the slightly frivolous ones and 1200 cases were objectively validated. A presentation of his work was done by Walter Semkin MD before the Society of Scientific Exploration. Stevenson's study found common attributes between the subjects and their counterparts like certain skills, birthmarks, similar diseases, and unusual behavior patterns and in many cases violent ends in the previous life.

Some of the common attributes in the study were:

The child communicates as soon as able to describe its previous life incidents

The child remembers details of its death usually a violent one

Based on the information provided by the child, his/her previous life events were verifiable after identifying the previous family

The scars and marks from the previous births appeared on the new life also, and the gender also remained same

Since reincarnation is a commonly accepted concept in India & Tibet, there has been a number of studies done in India towards verification of rebirth events. One of those books, is by one Pasricha "Claims of Reincarnation" where 60 cases were studied and documented for their authenticity.

Chapter 16

Ancient Super Humans & Miracle Men

So I have said enough about this because it is there and it is true. One explanation I can give for knowing this phenomenon, is to take our consciousness into a 3rd dimension. When this happens, one is able to see into the future and remember the past.

About 7000 BC, there lived in India a group of ascetics who were known as 'Rishis' These people were superhuman in many ways and could divine one's past and future. They had super listening skills and extraordinary memory power; they could remember a 20000 stanza poetry recited by their teacher and could repeat it from their memory! These 'Rishis' obtained full control of their minds and consciousness through severe austerity and penance. They could divine the future and past and were often called upon by the kings to advise them on the kingdom's problems. Some of them were also High Priests of the royal courts. The ordinary people who lived in those times often went to them for advice on their day to day problems. And their problems were solved by the ascetics.

The western world has not seen any miracles till the advent of Jesus around 2000 years back. But in India even around 500 years before the Christ, lived the Budha, who was an enlightened soul. He was able to see all his previous births and these events have been chronicled. Budhism was popular in India till the advent of Sankara, the great Hindu philosopher, who consolidated the Hindu religion with the Advaita Vedanta philosophy. He re-established Hinduism as the main religion of India, replacing Budhism, Jainism and other religions prevalent in India at that time. Budhism survived in other countries like Tibet, Srilanka,Japan, Korea, Cambodia, etc. through the Budha's disciples. Sankara performed many miracles including changing the course of a river, leaving his body and entering a King's body, and returning back (to his body). He crisscrossed India 3 times by foot. He wrote many poems and literature in Hinduism. He lived upto 32 years only.

Four-hundred years later Jesus appeared on the scene in the western world. He also lived 35 years like Sankara and did miracles.(compare his life with that of Sankara who also re-established Hinduism)All religions, except Hinduism, have one person who started them. Hinduism is called Anadi (Sanskrit) or of unknown origin. Their scriptures are the Vedas, which is the basis for the Sanatana Dharma (main concept in Hinduism). Many Rishies have jointly divined the

Vedas from space and given to the people. Ahimsa or non-violence is one of the tenets of Hinduism.

As recently as the 1950s, there lived in India an ascetic, who had the powers of knowing the past, and divining the future. He was the head of the Kanchi Mutt (one of the orders established by Adi Sankara). His name was Chandrasekhara Saraswati or Mahaperiyaval. He used to see thousands of devotees every day in his Matam (ashram) and changed many people's lives. When someone comes to him with a problem, he could divine their past life, and knew the karma that created the problem in their present life, and suggested a suitable remedy, that fixed the devotees problems. He gave new life to people who were dying of terminal illness. There are lots of testimonials in the U-tube from his devotees, and you can see them under Paramacharya of Kanchi Kamakoti. There have been books written about devotees' experiences, and he has a large following all over the world. In New Jersey, USA, there is a temple for him called Mani Mandapam.

I will recite a few incidents that happened to his devotees. (he does miracles even now after his death) One of his devotees, a doctor in Michigan, was going to work on a stormy icy day, when most of the roads were closed. A bridge leading to her hospital was snowed in and traffic was blocked. On her way, it started snowing heavily, and she was scared to drive her small car in the snow with no traction.

She called out to him to save her and became unconscious. After half hour, she woke up and found herself in her hospital parking lot. In her unconscious state, she was dreaming of her Guru taking control of her car. Her colleagues were amazed as to how she came to work in the snow-storm on the closed bridge.

I will recite one more instance of his miraculous deeds. One of the disciples had to go into a hospital because he lost his speech and could not walk. After some tests, the hospital determined he had a terminal illness, and they could not do anything for him. His brother called on his Guru for help. That night the patient had a dream of his Guru sitting on his bedside and telling him to get up and walk. Next, morning when his brother came to discharge him, they were all shocked to see him completely cured of his terminal illness. There are numerous other instances of his miracles. They are serialised in the Utube.

You remember, I talked about the Universal Law and Karma, which is an infallible principle of this law. There was another ascetic in India in the 1950s called Sathya Sai who could perform miracles; produce anything he wanted from his hand like ashes, gem stones, chains, etc for his devotees. He also remembered his past birth and announced what he will be born as in his next birth. When some devotee who had a physical ailment came to him, he used to cure him by taking on his karma, and he would be sick for days together till he got over that karma. This means that 'your Karma has to be worked out either in this or in some future life'; there is no escape from it. Once you understand this concept, you will think before doing anything negative. So you are incented to do good actions in this life. If everybody thinks about their karma, and the consequences thereof, then there will be less bad things in our lives. There are innumerable instances of divining past and future births by many Indian ascetics.

Chapter 17
Death, What Happens?

I am going to tell you now, about another important and not understood phenomenon of what happens when a person dies! This is a subject not understood by many people, because they have been told; that there is no life after death. When we accept there is transmigration of the soul, then we know that there is a next life after death. But most importantly, what happens when one dies? This information is hardly known. The Hindu scriptures have a view of this, as well as the Tibetan and other religions. But I want to believe in the Hindu view of it, as it has been discerned by the Hindu Rishis, who knew the past, present, and future; some of them have seen the soul leaving the body, moving from this life to the next. When the soul leaves the body, it is a very painful process. The life force Prana leaves through any of the many openings in the body like eyes, nose, and any other opening in the body. When the Prana, leaves the body, your form, which resides in your body, is ejected out of your body, and it hangs around you. Since the form has been living inside you and feels part of you, it tries to enter its body to which it belonged. It goes round and round your body and tries to enter the body lying in front of it. After some time, when it is not able to enter the body, because the Prana (the lifeforce) has left the body, it starts weeping. Especially, if the person who dies, has lots of attachment to life, some of those emotions are in the form, and it hangs around for a longer time. To show the form, that the body is not there anymore, the dead body is removed and cre-meated. The form when seeing the body burning, gets very distressed. That is why in the Hindu religion, there is a tradition of removing the body, and cremeated within 24 hours. This finds some kind of closure for the form

If the death is due to violent causes like accident, murder, etc. then it is all the more reason for the form to hang around in that place. This is one explanation, for the haunted houses, where the form of the dead person hangs around till it finds closure to the event. The priest class does a ceremony lasting 10 days to release the form, from this world. A stone image is setup, in which the form is invoked, and for 10 days, the form is offered food in the form of cooked rice balls and water. The idea is, everyday, the form increases in size after the feeding till the 10th day. On the 10th day it is released from the stone; on the 11th and 12th day, gifts are given to the bhramins to appease the form; and on the 13th day the house is cleaned, and all the relatives are invited for a feast, to celebrate the release of the dead person from the earthly connections.

You must be wondering what happened to the dead man's soul? Remember, the soul was lying hidden inside the body, eclipsed by the mind but witnessing everything that is happening to the person. As soon as the Prana leaves the body, it is gone into the upper layers, and under normal circumstances, it will incubate for some time, usually a year (as per the Hindu system). Here it will evaluate its past karma and determine where to take birth to fulfill its next round of karmas. This is true for a soul that has evolved to some extent. It has the luxury of incubating in the ether for as long as it desires for fully evolved souls till it decides on its next birth. Usually, these are purposeful births on earth for a specific objective. For others not so evolved, the incubation period is very short, and the soul is kicked back to the earth quickly, sometimes maybe in days. While coming down, this soul can accidentally latch on to one of the multiple Forms hanging around the earth, mostly negative ones; and therefore, will enter a body with it's attached baggage. So that person has to work out this additional karma in its life. This will explain why some are born in very negatively traited families like drug addicts, alcoholics, prisoners, from which they salvage themselves eventually.

I want to leave you with this simple truth, that if you understand the nature of the soul, that which, is in you, is in all beings, animals, birds, insects, etc. If you understand this truth, then you will see no difference between black and white, rich and poor, the homeless, the marginalized humans in this world in whom the same soul resides. This understanding will help you develop Compassion and Love towards other human beings. Love will bring Joy, Happiness, and Peace in your life.

Love will overcome all obstacles in life. If you practice this eventually, it will become unconditional love, which will bring everlasting Joy and Happiness in life!

I hope I have given you an insight into the workings of the mind, soul, past life, life after death, etc. With this, Lawrence ended the session.

When I awoke, next morning from my couch where I had fallen asleep, I saw Lawrence cuddled in front of me. I thought he was still sleeping, when I nudged him, his head turned the other side. I realized he was not breathing, and I called an ambulance and the medics who came checked him said he had been dead for a while in his sleep. I thought he came to give me a specific message about animal cruelty and knowledge about past life, soul, etc. Once his message had been delivered, his purpose in this life was over and he went on to his next life.

I wanted to use the knowledge, especially the cruelty to animals part, by joining the humane society and working towards that goal with other people.

Glossary

Many terms used in this book is of Sanskrit (ancient Vedic language of India) origin. I give below the meaning of some of them.

Consciousness: Hidden force inside one's body

Chakras: Imaginary nodes in the body where the channels meet, 7 in number.

Jiva: The individual soul residing in one's body

Prana: Term for life force belonging to an individual moving through the channels

Lung: Tibetan word for life force

Reincarnation: Reborn into next life after death in this life

Rishis: A class of superhumans who lived in India about 5000 years ago.

Vasanas: Character attributes that are part of one's personality carried into next life.

Vedas: Ancient Indian language on which Hindu scriptures are based

Lightning Source UK Ltd.
Milton Keynes UK
UKHW021225171220
375421UK00008B/442